Doggone It!

D0503264

For the *real* Pepper . . . *AROOOOOO!*

Text copyright © 2003 by Nancy Krulik. Illustrations copyright
© 2003 by John and Wendy. All rights reserved. Published by
Grosset & Dunlap, a division of Penguin Young Readers Group,
345 Hudson Street, New York, NY, 10014. GROSSET & DUNLAP
is a trademark of Penguin Group (USA) Inc. Published
simultaneously in Canada. Printed in U.S.A.

Library of Congress Cataloging-in-Publication Data

Krulik, Nancy E.
  Doggone it! / by Nancy Krulik ; illustrated by John & Wendy.
       p. cm. — (Katie Kazoo, switcheroo ; 8)
Summary: When strict Mrs. Derkman moves next door to third-
grader Katie Carew, scares her friends away, and insists she keep
her dog, Pepper, on a leash, Katie finds a non-magical solution to
the problem. Includes steps for teaching a dog to sit and stay.
  [1. Neighbors—Fiction. 2. Dogs—Fiction. 3. Teachers—Fiction.
4. Magic—Fiction.] I. John & Wendy, ill. II. Title.
  PZ7.K944Dn 2005
  [Fic]—dc21
                                                    2003005213

        ISBN 0-448-43172-6   G H I J   ·

KATIE KAZOO, SWITCHEROO

Doggone It!

by Nancy Krulik • illustrated by John & Wendy

Grosset & Dunlap

Chapter 1

"Are they here yet?" Jeremy Fox asked, as he rode his bike up to Katie Carew's house early Saturday morning.

Katie was sitting on the front porch with her dog, Pepper. *Waiting.*

"Nope." Katie told her best friend. "And I've been sitting here all morning."

"You still don't know anything about the new neighbors?" Jeremy plopped down beside her. "I thought your parents met them already."

Katie shook her head. "My mom won't even give me a hint about what they're like. She thinks it's better if I'm surprised."

"That's *so* not fair," Jeremy said.

"I hope they have a lot of kids," Katie thought out loud.

Just then, Katie's other best friend, Suzanne Lock, came skipping rope around the corner. As she reached Katie's house, Suzanne put down her jump rope and glared at Jeremy. "What are you doing here?" she demanded.

"Waiting for Katie's new neighbors."

Suzanne turned to Katie. "I thought *we* were going to meet your new neighbors together."

"We are," Katie assured her other best friend. "Jeremy wants to see them, too."

"Three's a crowd," Suzanne complained.

"So leave," Jeremy told her.

Katie shook her head. She liked both of her best friends so much. It was too bad they couldn't like each other. "Come on, you guys," she said. "This is a really important day. There's a new family moving in next door."

"I hope they have a teenage girl," Suzanne told Katie. "Then we can find out about the newest music and clothes before anyone else. Teenagers know all about that kind of stuff."

Jeremy scowled. "Who needs another teenage girl around here? I'd rather have a couple of new boys in the neighborhood." He stopped and thought for a moment. "Maybe they'll put up a basketball hoop over their garage."

"Girls play basketball, too," Katie reminded him.

"Yeah," Suzanne added. "Ever hear of the WNBA?"

"You're right," Jeremy admitted. "But we just got a new girl in the neighborhood."

"You mean Becky?" Katie asked him. Becky Stern had moved to Cherrydale from Atlanta about two months ago. But she already had so many friends that it was weird to think of her as the "new girl."

"Becky, your *girlfriend*," Suzanne added with a giggle.

Jeremy turned beet red. "She is *not* my girlfriend," he insisted. "Take that back."

But Suzanne wouldn't give in. "Jeremy and

Becky sitting in a tree, K-I-S-S-I-N-G," she sang. "First comes love. Then comes marriage. Then comes little Jeremy in a baby carriage. Sucking his thumb, wetting his pants, doing the hootchie-cootchie dance!"

Now Jeremy was really mad. "She is *not* my girlfriend," he insisted.

"She wishes she was," Suzanne told him. "Everyone knows it."

"That's not my problem," Jeremy said. He blushed again.

"I wonder if the new family will have a dog," Katie said, quickly changing the subject. "Pepper would like that."

"*Arf!*" At the sound of his name, the chocolate-and-white cocker spaniel looked up at Katie and smiled.

"See?" Katie asked. She kissed her dog on the head. "He'd love a four-legged friend."

"Yeah, but what if the new family has a cat?" Suzanne asked. "That wouldn't be so great."

"Why not? Pepper can be friends with a cat."

Jeremy shook his head at that. "A cat and a dog? I don't know, Katie."

"Pepper's not like other dogs," Katie insisted. "He's special."

Before anyone could argue with that, a huge white moving van came rumbling down the street.

"They're here!" Katie yelled excitedly.

Suzanne stood up and fixed her hair. "How do I look?" she asked.

The kids all watched as two big men got out of the van and began to unload the new neighbors' belongings. Before long there were chairs, tables, lamps, and a big wooden bed on the front lawn.

"I don't see any toys," Katie said nervously.

"They're probably packed away in boxes," Jeremy reasoned.

Just then, a red car pulled into the driveway beside the house.

"That's the new family!" Katie cheered. "Let's go meet them." She started to run over toward the car.

Katie didn't get very far. She stopped dead in her tracks and stared, as a woman with dark, short hair and small, round glasses got out of the car. She looked really familiar.

Frighteningly familiar!

"It can't be . . . " Suzanne began.

"I think it is," Jeremy told her. He looked again. "Oh yeah. It's her, all right."

"Oh no!" Katie cried out. "This is awful!"

Chapter 2

There was no doubt about it. The woman who had gotten out of the car was Mrs. Derkman, Katie's third-grade teacher—*strict* Mrs. Derkman, the teacher with the most rules in the whole school.

"Suzanne, can you believe how horrible this is?" Katie exclaimed.

Suzanne didn't answer. She just stood there with her mouth wide open as Mrs. Derkman walked toward the kids.

"*You* bought the house next to mine?" Katie asked in disbelief.

"Didn't your mother tell you?" Mrs. Derkman replied.

"I um . . . she . . . I think she wanted it to be a surprise," Katie stammered.

"And we are *definitely* surprised!" Jeremy said.

"I can tell." Mrs. Derkman laughed. "Suzanne, please close your mouth before a bug flies down your throat."

"Barbara, which of these boxes goes in the bathroom?" Mr. Derkman called to his wife.

Barbara? Katie had never thought of Mrs. Derkman as someone with a first name before.

"Well, I'd better get to work. I have a whole house to unpack." Mrs. Derkman smiled at Katie. "We'll talk later, *neighbor*."

"Yes, Mrs. Derkman," Katie answered quietly.

As Mrs. Derkman headed toward her new house, Jeremy strapped on his helmet and walked over to his bike.

"I . . . well . . . I gotta get home," he said nervously.

"Don't you want to play ball or something?" Katie asked him.

Jeremy looked at Mrs. Derkman and her husband. They were on their front porch, watching the movers. "Not today, Katie," Jeremy told her. "Maybe we can play tomorrow . . . at *my* house."

As Jeremy rode off, Katie smiled at Suzanne. "I'll go get my jump rope. We can make up some new rhymes or something."

Suzanne picked up her rope. "Uh, I have to be getting home," she told Katie nervously.

"It's getting late."

Katie looked at her friend. "Late for what?"

"Um, um . . . I just have to go," Suzanne said.

Katie looked down at Pepper. "At least *you* still want to play with me, don't you, boy?" she asked, scratching the spaniel between the ears.

Crash! One of the movers dropped a heavy box on the lawn. The loud noise scared Pepper. He turned and ran inside as fast he could.

Next door, Mrs. Derkman was yelling at the movers. She sounded angry and impatient— just the way she did when the kids in class 3A wouldn't listen.

"This is a nightmare!" Katie exclaimed.

Chapter 3

"Would you like some more carrots?"
Katie's mother asked at dinner that night.

"No thanks," Katie mumbled.

"But you've hardly eaten a thing," Mrs.
Carew said. "I made all your favorites—veggie
burgers, carrots, and mashed potatoes."

Katie sighed. Veggie burgers were her
favorite. But she didn't feel much like eating.

"I'm not hungry," she mumbled.

"Well, I'll have some more carrots—and
potatoes, too," Katie's dad said, patting his
stomach. "This is a great dinner."

Katie's mother smiled. "Speaking of
dinner, I was thinking we should invite the

Derkmans for a barbecue tomorrow. They've probably been too busy unpacking to cook."

Katie gulped. Mrs. Derkman? Eating at her house? How horrible was that?

"No!" Katie shouted out suddenly.

Her mother looked surprised. "What do you mean 'no'?"

Katie sighed. Didn't her mother understand *anything?* "Mom, Mrs. Derkman is my teacher. I can't have dinner with her."

"Katie, that's silly. The Derkmans just moved in. We should be neighborly," her mother said firmly.

"There are a gazillion houses." Katie moaned. "Why did they have to pick the one right next door to us? I wish . . . "

Katie was about to say that she wished anyone else in the whole world had moved in next door, but she stopped herself. Katie knew better than to make wishes like that. It was too dangerous.

Katie had learned all about wishes after one really bad day at school. She'd lost thefootball game for her team, ruined her favorite jeans, and burped in front of the whole class. That day, Katie had wished that she could be anyone but herself.

There must have been a shooting star flying overhead or something when she made that wish, because the very next day the magic wind came.

The magic wind was a really wild storm that seemed to blow only around Katie. The magic wind was really powerful. So powerful, in fact, that it was able to turn Katie into somebody else.

The first time the magic wind came, it changed Katie into Speedy, the class hamster.

She'd spent a whole morning running around trying to keep from getting stepped on.

Luckily, Katie had changed back into herself before anyone realized who the class hamster really was.

The magic wind didn't only turn Katie into animals. Sometimes it turned her into grown-ups, like Lucille, the school lunch lady, and Mr. Kane, the principal.

Other times, the magic wind turned Katie into other kids, like Suzanne's baby sister, Heather, or Becky Stern, the new girl in school. Once it had actually switcherooed her into Jeremy Fox. Katie didn't like being a boy at all. She wasn't even sure which bathroom she was supposed to go into!

That's why Katie didn't make wishes anymore. When they came true, things never turned out the way she hoped they would. The truth was, Mrs. Derkman was her neighbor, and there was nothing Katie could do.

But that didn't mean she had to like it.

Chapter 4

Slurp. Katie was fast asleep when she felt a wet lick on her face. She opened her eyes slowly and came face-to-face with Pepper. As soon as Katie opened her eyes, the spaniel's brown stubby tail began wagging wildly.

Katie glanced at the clock on her wall. It was only 7:15. "Didn't anybody tell you it's Sunday?" she moaned to her dog.

Pepper answered with a big, soggy lick to her nose.

"Okay, okay," she giggled. "You win. Let's go play."

Just then, Katie heard someone singing loudly outside. Whoever it was had a terrible voice—high and screechy, like fingernails on a blackboard.

Pepper growled.

"Who could that be?" Katie wondered aloud as she put on her clothes. Quickly, she brushed her teeth and raced outside to find out what was going on.

Whoa! What a surprise!

When Katie and Pepper walked out into Katie's front yard, they discovered Mrs. Derkman working in her garden. The teacher was wearing a huge straw hat and a pair of overalls. Her hands were covered with green gardening gloves. And as if that weren't weird enough . . .

Mrs. Derkman was singing at the top of her lungs.

"Noah, he built them, he built them an arky-arky," the teacher screeched.

Katie couldn't believe that this was the same Mrs. Derkman who was her teacher. Mrs. Derkman never wore anything other

than neat dresses and sensible shoes. And she never—*ever*— sang out loud.

"Made it out of hickory barky-barky . . . " Mrs. Derkman croaked.

Katie choked back a laugh.

"*Ruff! Ruff!*" Pepper came racing over to Katie with a yellow tennis ball in his mouth. He wanted to play.

"Okay, boy," Katie said with a smile. She took the soggy ball and flung it across the lawn. "Fetch!"

Unfortunately, Katie's aim wasn't very good. The ball flew into Mrs. Derkman's garden. Pepper leaped right into the flowerbed and caught the ball in his mouth.

"Oh, no! Not my pansies!" Mrs. Derkman waved her arms wildly. "Get out of here, you rotten dog!"

Pepper cocked his head curiously to the side. He'd just caught the ball in the air. Usually somebody said "good dog" after he did that. Sometimes he even got a treat.

But Mrs. Derkman certainly wasn't about to give Pepper a treat.

Katie walked over to Mrs. Derkman's house. "Sorry about that," she said shyly.

"My new flowerbed." Mrs. Derkman moaned. "Katie, could you please keep this dog on your lawn from now on?"

"His name is Pepper," Katie told her.

Mrs. Derkman took a deep breath. "Okay, could you please keep Pepper on your lawn?"

Katie nodded. "I'm sorry about your flowers."

"It's okay," Mrs. Derkman said. "Just please keep *Pepper* out of my garden. I've planted a new strawberry patch and some tomato plants. They have to be treated very tenderly. Don't they, Sven?"

Sven? Katie looked around. "Who are you talking to?" she asked her teacher curiously.

Mrs. Derkman laughed. "Sven," she said, pointing to the big stone troll standing in the middle of the garden. "We've had him for years. I found him when I was visiting

Norway, and I just fell in love with him."

Katie looked at the troll. It had a pointy red hat and a creepy smile on its face. It definitely wasn't loveable!

"I talk to Sven all the time," Mrs. Derkman continued. "It's a kind of game I play to pass the time while I'm working in the garden."

How weird is that? Katie wondered to herself.

"I love gardening!" Mrs. Derkman told Katie. "I spend every hour I can out here with my little babies." Mrs. Derkman ran her hand lovingly over one of her pansies.

"It seems like a lot of work," Katie said.

Mrs. Derkman nodded. "It is. But I don't mind. My plants are worth it. I water them and fertilize them. They especially love when I sing to them."

For a minute, Katie thought her teacher was going to burst into song once again. Luckily, at just that second, Mr. Derkman came out onto the porch. He was wearing a red flannel bathrobe. His long, hairy legs stuck out from under the robe.

"Hi, Katie," Mr. Derkman said, waving. He looked down at Pepper. "Cute dog. He's a cocker spaniel right?"

Katie nodded.

"I had a beagle when I was growing up," Mr. Derkman recalled. "Barbara, isn't it wonderful to have a cute dog living right next door?"

Mrs. Derkman rolled her eyes. "Wonderful," she said sarcastically.

Mr. Derkman held out a big mug. "Snookums, your coffee is ready," he told his wife.

Mrs. Derkman stood and wiped some dirt from her overalls. "Okay, Freddy Bear," she said. "I'll be right in."

Snookums? Freddy Bear? Katie couldn't wait to tell the kids at school about this!

On second thought, they'd probably never believe her.

Chapter 5

The moment Katie walked onto the playground on Monday morning, she was surrounded by the other kids from class 3A.

"Suzanne told us Mrs. Derkman moved in next door to you," Zoe Canter said. "Is it true?"

Katie nodded.

"I told you so," Suzanne told the kids. "I was right there with her when Mrs. Derkman drove up."

"Hey, I was there, too," Jeremy announced. "I was there *first*."

"Jeremy you're such a good friend," Becky Stern said. She smiled brightly at him.

Jeremy blushed.

"Oh, Katie!" Miriam Chan exclaimed. "I'm so sorry."

"What's it like living next door to a teacher?" Becky asked.

"It's awful," Suzanne butted in. "Isn't it, Katie?"

"It's definitely horrible," Katie agreed. "I

mean, last night, Mrs. Derkman and her husband came over for a barbecue. How embarrassing is that?"

"Mrs. Derkman came to your house?" Kevin Camilleri asked with surprise.

Katie nodded. "Mr. Derkman brought his ukulele. He played songs, and Mrs. Derkman danced."

Jeremy's eyes opened wide. "Mrs. Derkman *danced?*"

Katie nodded. "You should have seen her. She was doing a Hawaiian hula."

The kids all tried to picture their teacher wiggling her hips in Katie's backyard. But they couldn't. It was too weird to even imagine.

"You had to be there," Katie told them. "It was gross. But not as gross as the strawberry pie she baked. That was all burnt."

"I can't eat strawberries," Mandy Banks said. "I'm allergic to them."

"I'm allergic to *Mrs. Derkman*. I feel so bad

for you, Katie Kazoo," George Brennan said, using the special nickname he'd made up for Katie.

George and Mrs. Derkman did not get along well at all. George told a lot of jokes. Mrs. Derkman didn't like any kidding around in her classroom. "I knew you would understand how I feel," Katie said. "You'd definitely hate living next door to Mrs. Derkman."

"I hate living on the same *planet* as Mrs. Derkman," George agreed.

Katie looked at Kevin. "It wouldn't be so bad for you, though, Kevin," Katie told him. "She's got tomato plants in her garden."

Kevin couldn't believe it. His teacher was growing his favorite food in her garden. "Do you think she'll bring tomatoes to school?" he asked.

"I wouldn't eat them, Kev," George said. "What if she's like that witch in *Snow White?* One bite of a Derkman tomato and you'll sleep until a girl kisses you." George pretended to faint.

"You guys should see this garden," Katie continued. "It's huge. And in the middle, she has this ugly troll statue—that she *talks* to! It's the creepiest thing I ever saw."

"Mrs. Derkman is the creepiest thing *I* ever saw," George joked.

"Do you think Mrs. Derkman will treat you special now that she's your neighbor?" Zoe asked Katie. "Maybe she'll give you less homework or let you go to the bathroom whenever you want."

"I don't know," Katie said. "Do you think she'd do that?"

"It would be the *least* she could do," Suzanne assured her.

Hmmm. Katie smiled. Maybe there was a bright side to this whole mess after all.

Chapter 6

Or maybe there wasn't a bright side.

"What good is it having a teacher live next door if she's still mean?" Katie exclaimed that night, as she and her parents sat together in the living room. "I think she was stricter with me today than she was with anyone else."

Mrs. Carew put her arm around her daughter. "I know it's kind of strange having her as your neighbor. But I'm sure she isn't treating you any worse because of it."

"Yes, she is," Katie insisted. "Today she called on me when she was sure I didn't know the answer. And she wouldn't let me go to the bathroom until Suzanne came back."

"But Mrs. Derkman always does things like that," Mrs. Carew said. "She hasn't changed
at all."

Katie frowned.

Mr. Carew reached into his pocket and pulled out a small, white envelope. "Speaking of Mrs. Derkman, I found this in the mailbox today. It's from her."

Katie gulped. A note from her teacher! This could be really bad.

"What does it say?" Katie's mom asked.

"Dear Mr. and Mrs. Carew," Katie's dad read out loud. "I am writing to tell you that your dog ate all the strawberries from my plants. From now on, please keep your dog on a leash. If you insist on letting him run wild, I will have to call the authorities. Sincerely, Barbara Derkman."

Now Katie was really mad. "Pepper would never eat her strawberries," she insisted.

"I know," Katie's dad agreed. "But some

dog must have."

"Then put *that* dog on a leash," Katie said.

Mrs. Carew put her arm around Katie.

"We'll put Pepper on a leash for a few days.

Then, when Mrs. Derkman finds out who's really eating her strawberries, things can go back to normal."

"But Pepper's lived here for years. He's hardly ever been on a leash, and he's never caused any trouble." Katie thought for a minute. "In fact, there weren't any problems in this neighborhood before Mrs. Derkman moved here. Maybe *she's* the one who needs to be walked on a leash!"

"Katie, I'm sorry, but Pepper's going to have to be on a leash for a while. Just until we can clear his good name," Mrs. Carew said.

"It won't be so bad," Katie's dad added. "We'll get Pepper one of those leashes with plastic jewels on it. He'll feel like a movie star."

Katie looked lovingly at Pepper. He was a good dog. All the kids liked him. That was more than she could say about Mrs. Derkman.

It just wasn't fair.

Chapter 7

The next day, Suzanne, Jeremy, Becky, and George walked Katie home from school. They were trying to cheer her up. But nothing they said or did could make Katie feel better.

She would never feel better again. At least, not as long as Mrs. Derkman was around.

Luckily, when the kids reached Katie's house, Mrs. Derkman *wasn't* around. Her car wasn't in the driveway, and the lights were all off inside the house.

"Hey, she's not here!" Katie exclaimed. "You guys want to stay for a while? Maybe play tag or something?"

"Well, as long as Mrs. *Jerk*man's not

around . . . " George began.

That was all Jeremy needed to hear. "Tag! You're it!" he shouted, as he tapped George on the shoulder.

George didn't try racing back after Jeremy. It would be easier to tag Katie.

"Watch out, Katie Kazoo!" George shouted across the lawn. "Here I come!"

Katie took off like a rocket, trying to dodge George's outstretched arm. She smiled as she soared across her front lawn. Tag was Katie's favorite game.

But as she looked up toward her house, Katie's smile turned to a frown. She could see Pepper sitting in the front hall. His little

brown-and-white face was pressed up against the screen door.

Usually Pepper played tag, too. He would run on the lawn with the kids, barking happily and wagging his tail.

But that was before Mrs. Derkman moved in next door.

"Gotcha!" George shouted, tagging Katie on the shoulder. "Boy, you're easy, Katie Kazoo!"

Katie sighed. She wasn't *always* that easy to catch. She just hadn't been paying attention.

She was now. "Better run, George!" she said. "I'm going to tag you back!"

"Oh, come on." George moaned. "Everyone always gets me. You haven't tagged Suzanne or Becky yet."

Katie darted off in search of Suzanne. But before she could reach her friend, a familiar, angry voice rang out from the sidewalk.

"Katie! Be careful. You almost stepped on

my petunias!" Mrs. Derkman, shouted as she zoomed down the block on a shiny silver scooter. The teacher stopped right in front of Katie's house and took off her yellow-and-pink helmet.

The kids all stared at her. They'd never

seen their teacher on a scooter before.

"I hope you've all finished your math homework," Mrs. Derkman added strictly.

Jeremy, Suzanne, Becky, and George looked at each other nervously. Finished? They hadn't even *started* their math homework.

"I gotta go," George said suddenly.

"Me, too," Jeremy agreed. "I'll see you tomorrow, Katie." He ran off after George.

"Wait up, Jeremy," Becky called out in her thick southern accent. "I'm going your way." She ran off after him.

"I guess I have to go do my homework, too," Suzanne said.

Katie frowned. "Mrs. Derkman is ruining my life!"

Suzanne nodded. "I know. She's really mean." Suzanne looked over at Mrs. Derkman's house. The teacher was standing on the porch, watching the girls. "I wish I could stay and keep you company, but I really gotta go." Suzanne said.

Katie shrugged. "It's okay. I have to take Pepper for his walk, anyhow."

"How's that leash thing going?"

"Lousy," Katie said. "Pepper hates it. My mom says he'll get used to it, but I don't think so."

As Suzanne walked away, Katie went inside to get Pepper's leash. She hooked it onto his collar and led him outside.

Katie was careful not to walk Pepper anywhere near Mrs. Derkman's lawn. The teacher had gone inside, but you never knew. Maybe she was spying on Katie through a window or something.

"I'm really sorry, Pepper," she said as led him down the block.

Pepper looked up at Katie with sad, brown eyes. He let out a little whimper. It was the only sound on the whole block. There was no one else around. Mrs. Derkman had made sure of that.

Katie didn't blame her friends for not wanting to play at her house. She didn't even like playing there anymore.

Katie sat down at the curb and petted Pepper's sad little head. Pepper reached up and gently licked her face. He knew it wasn't her fault.

Just then a cool breeze brushed against the back of Katie's neck. It started out gentle

enough, but within seconds, the breeze turned into a strong wind—a wind that was blowing only around Katie.

The magic wind was back!

As the wild tornado swirled faster and faster, Katie let go of Pepper's leash. She didn't want him to get stuck in her own private storm. "Run, Pepper, run!" she shouted, as the wind blew stronger and stronger.

And then, suddenly, it stopped. Just like that.

Slowly Katie opened her eyes. She looked around. Everything was sort of gray and dull.

Frantically, she searched for Pepper. She didn't see the cocker spaniel anywhere.

Katie gulped nervously. Had he gotten out of the way in time? Or had the magic wind blown him far from home?

Katie sniffed the ground beside her. Oh, good. She could smell Pepper nearby. He was safe.

Katie sniffed again. This time, Pepper's scent mixed in the air with the smell of a barbecue being lit. Someone was grilling hamburgers.

Yum! They smelled delicious.

Wait a minute. I don't eat hamburgers, Katie thought to herself. *I'm a vegetarian.*

Still, those burgers sure did smell good. Katie just had to have one. Quickly, she scampered off in the direction of the barbecue. As she ran, her stubby brown tail wagged wildly.

Her *tail?*

Oh no! Katie had turned into a dog.

Katie looked at her body. She was chocolate brown and white. The fur on her paws was soft and curly. And her long ears waved back and forth as she turned her head.

Katie hadn't turned into just any dog—she'd turned into Pepper!

Chapter 8

Katie sat back on her hind legs and looked at the world through Pepper's eyes. Everything seemed yellow, blue, and gray. Katie knew the stop sign on the corner should be red, but to her it looked pale yellow. The sign was sort of blurry, too. It was hard to see something so far away.

Katie was frightened. She really wanted to go home, run into her room, and hide under her bed until the magic wind came and changed her back.

Katie looked out in front of her. It was strange being so low to the ground. All she saw were the bottoms of things—tree trunks, sign posts, and . . . *a fire hydrant.*

For some reason, the sight of the hydrant made Katie's tail wag wildly. She scampered over as quickly as she could and began to sniff.

Lots of dogs had been there before her. And every one of them had peed on the hydrant. Their stinky smells were everywhere.

Yuck! Katie thought to herself. But she couldn't stop herself from smelling. It was a dog thing.

Sniff, sniff. A big dog had visited the hydrant. Probably a German Shepherd.

Sniff, sniff. There'd been a little dog there as well. *Really* little, like a Chihuahua or something.

Katie wanted to leave her mark, too. She picked up her hind leg and left a puddle. Then she dug wildly at the dirt under her feet. There. Now all the other dogs would know she'd been there.

When she was through peeing and digging, Katie decided to head for home. She didn't get very far, however, before a sweet, fruity smell reached her nose. There, in the middle of the sidewalk, was a half-chewed blueberry bagel.

Mmmm. People food.

I shouldn't eat that, Katie told herself. Who knows where its been. She sniffed at the bagel. It smelled so good, she couldn't help herself.

Crunch. She snatched up the treat and started to chew.

This is so gross, Katie thought, as bits of sidewalk sand and dirt scratched against her tongue. But she didn't spit the bagel out. It tasted too good.

Katie's stubby little tail wagged happily back and forth as she ate. "I wonder if I can catch that?" she barked to herself as she swallowed the last bit of dirty bagel.

Katie turned toward her tail and stretched her neck back. Her tail was still very far away. She reached farther back. She began turning around and around in a circle, as she tried to grab her tail.

Whooaa, I'm getting dizzy, Katie thought as she spun.

Still, she didn't stop. She was determined to chase her tail—although she wasn't quite sure what she would do with it if she caught it.

Boy, dogs sure do weird things, she thought.

Just then, Katie heard a squeaky chattering noise. She sat still and quietly.

The noise seemed to be coming from a

nearby oak tree. Katie put her nose to the
ground and sniffed. Her tail began to wag
wildly.

Oh boy! *SQUIRREL*!

Katie darted off toward the oak tree. But
the squirrel was quicker. He scrambled up the
tree trunk.

The squirrel was high in the tree—too
high for Katie to ever reach him. But that
didn't stop her from trying. She leaped up and
down at the base of the tree, barking wildly.

The squirrel sat on its high branch,
chattering away. That rotten rodent was
laughing at Katie.

Plink. An acorn landed on Katie's nose.
The squirrel laughed harder.

Now Katie was really mad. She jumped higher. She barked louder.

The squirrel just kept on laughing.

Finally, Katie gave up. She wasn't going to catch the squirrel . . . at least not now.

I'll be back! Katie gave one last bark and started for home.

Just as Katie reached her front porch, she heard a loud, high-pitched dog yelp. It was coming from Mrs. Derkman's yard.

From the sound of the bark, Katie could tell this was a really small dog. But that didn't mean anything. Even small dogs could be mean. They had sharp teeth, and they weren't afraid to use them—especially if they thought a bigger dog was in their territory.

Katie sat still, watching.

Chapter 9

Katie's brown-and-white doggie eyes grew large as she watched with surprise at what happened next.

The little white dog took a big bite of one Mrs. Derkman's cucumbers! The white dog was the mysterious fruit and vegetable thief!

Unfortunately, Mrs. Derkman didn't know about the white dog. She was sure to blame the missing cucumber on Pepper. She was going to say he'd been running loose again.

Which he was . . . sort of. But it wasn't Katie's fault. It was the magic wind's fault.

There was no way Katie could explain that to Mrs. Derkman. The teacher would never

believe that Katie had actually turned into
her own dog!

"*Grrrr!*" Katie let out a loud, frustrated
growl.

The scraggly pup looked up in fear. Her
ears stood straight up on her head. She
sniffed around nervously. Then she began to
whimper.

Oh no! Katie had made the puppy cry.

"Calm down, little puppy," Katie whispered
softly.

But the puppy kept crying.

Katie had to let the white dog know that she wanted to be friends. She padded over and gave the pup a real doggie greeting: she sniffed at the dog's rear end. That was the way dogs said "hello."

The puppy's tail began to wag happily. Katie sniffed again. *Pew*. The dog's bottom smelled awful.

"I'm glad people don't say hello this way," Katie told herself as she sniffed even harder. "It's gross!"

The puppy was so happy to have a friend. She jumped up and let out a little squeal of joy. Then she turned around and nipped at Katie's nose. Lucky for Katie, the dog still had her puppy teeth.

Katie wondered where this scraggly white dog had come from. She didn't have a collar or tags. She was very skinny, and she smelled like she'd never had a bath in her whole life.

Katie didn't have a lot of time to feel bad for the puppy. Suddenly, she heard chattering

noises coming from a nearby tree.

Katie would know that sound anywhere—the squirrel was back!

This time, she was going to get that furry-tailed acorn thrower!

Without thinking, Katie took off after the squirrel. She kept her eyes on him the whole time—which is why she didn't notice the statue in the middle of the garden.

Bam! Katie ran right into Mrs. Derkman's beloved troll. The troll fell backward and bashed its head on a rock. The top of its pointy red hat crumbled into a thousand pieces.

As if that weren't bad enough, the squirrel got away. It was sitting on a high branch, laughing. Katie leaped up on the tree and barked wildly.

Katie's angry shouts scared the little puppy. She let out a big yelp and raced off.

"Come back!" Katie barked to the dog. "I can help you!"

The scrawny white pup didn't seem to hear Katie barking. But Mrs. Derkman did. She came running to find out what the all the noise was about.

Mrs. Derkman didn't see the little puppy that had been eating her cucumbers. She didn't see the squirrel laughing in the tree.

All the teacher saw was Pepper sitting in the middle of her tomato plants.

"Get out of here, you trouble-making dog!" she shouted.

Katie didn't have to be told twice. She ran off as fast as her four legs could carry her.

Chapter 10

Katie sat, huddled against the side of her house. Her little brown-and-white body shook with fear. She whimpered sadly.

Pepper was in really big trouble. And it was all Katie's fault.

Katie recognized the sound of Mrs. Derkman's footsteps as the teacher raced up the front steps of the Carew house. "I've had it with that mutt," Mrs. Derkman muttered angrily to herself.

Katie listened as her mother opened the door of their house. "Mrs. Derkman, what a nice surprise," she heard her mother say.

"Well, you're half right," Mrs. Derkman

answered. "There have been a few surprises today. But none of them have been nice."

Katie gulped.

Unfortunately, Katie didn't get to hear any more of the conversation. The sudden whistling of strong winds blocked out any other sounds.

Wow. It felt like there was a real storm coming.

Katie looked around nervously. The leaves on the trees were still. The clouds in the sky didn't seem to be moving, either. The wild winds were only blowing around Katie.

The magic wind was back!

As the gusts swirled around her, Katie began to howl in fear. The tornado-like winds

were very strong, and she was very small. What if the winds picked her up and carried her someplace far away? Would she ever be able to find her way home?

Katie curled her body into a frightened ball. She covered her eyes with her front paws and waited.

There was nothing else she could do. She couldn't stop the magic wind. It had to stop itself.

And that's exactly what happened. The magic wind stopped blowing, just as suddenly as it had begun. Katie slowly lifted her hands from her eyes. She looked around. Everything seemed clear and bright.

She stared down at her feet. There were her red sneakers. *Stop-sign* red.

She stared at her arms. There were five fingers on each hand . . . and no sign of fur anywhere.

Katie Kazoo was back!

So was Pepper. The cocker spaniel rubbed his furry body against Katie's legs.

"I'm so sorry, Pepper," Katie said. "I didn't mean to get you in trouble." She took Pepper's leash and slowly began to lead him toward her front porch.

Mrs. Derkman was just leaving. As she spotted Katie and Pepper, the teacher's mouth twisted into a tight frown. Her eyes bugged. Her cheeks turned red. She looked as though her head might explode!

Katie was sure Mrs. Derkman was going to scream at her. But the teacher didn't say a word. She just stormed back home.

Chapter 11

"It's just awful, Suzanne," Katie said into the phone later that night. "Mrs. Derkman was yelling at my mom."

"Mrs. Derkman shouts all the time," Suzanne reminded her. "Ask George. She's *always* yelling at him."

"But not like this," Katie explained. "She said if she ever caught Pepper on her lawn again, she would call the dog catcher!"

"Wow," Suzanne said. "That *is* really bad."

"I know," Katie agreed. "Mrs. Derkman told my mother to build a fence around our yard. That way, she could be sure Pepper would never get into her garden again."

"What did your mom say?"

"She told Mrs. Derkman we couldn't afford to do that," Katie said. "But Mrs. Derkman didn't care."

"So what are you going to do?" Suzanne asked. "Can you keep Pepper from eating her vegetables?"

Katie frowned. Even her best friend believed Pepper was the veggie thief. "It isn't Pepper."

Suzanne sighed. "Katie, I know you love Pepper and all, but maybe he *is* eating them.

You said Mrs. Derkman caught him right in the yard. And he did break her troll."

"That wasn't his fault," Katie said. "He was chasing this really mean squirrel."

Suzanne laughed. "Come on, Katie, are you saying it was the squirrel's fault?"

"Yes!" Katie exclaimed. "You don't know this squirrel. He's a tease. He laughs at Pepper and throws acorns at him, and . . ." Katie stopped in the middle of her sentence. She knew she was telling the truth.

She also knew Suzanne would never believe her.

"Anyway, Pepper isn't the one eating her vegetables," Katie continued. "It's this little white puppy. I saw her."

"Did someone on your block get a puppy?" Suzanne asked excitedly.

"No. I think she's a stray. And you can bet if Mrs. Derkman sees the puppy on her lawn, she's going to call the dog catcher."

"Oh, the poor puppy," Suzanne said.

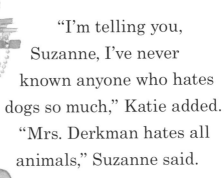

"I'm telling you, Suzanne, I've never known anyone who hates dogs so much," Katie added.

"Mrs. Derkman hates all animals," Suzanne said. "She doesn't go near Speedy's cage since he got loose that time." Katie giggled to herself. She knew all about that. After all, she'd *been* Speedy that morning. Katie would never forget the look of fear in Mrs. Derkman's eyes when she saw the class hamster running across the floor.

"I'll bet Mrs. Derkman never had a pet when she was growing up," Suzanne continued. "No one who ever had a pet could hate animals this much."

"Suzanne, you're a genius!" Katie exclaimed suddenly.

"I know," Suzanne agreed. Then she stopped for a minute. "*Why* am I genius?" she asked curiously.

"You've just solved Pepper's problem."

"I have?" Suzanne asked.

"Yes," Katie said. "But it's going to take a lot of work. Will you help me?"

"Sure," Suzanne agreed. "What do you want me to do?"

"The first thing you need to do is talk your mom into letting us use your basement for a few days." Katie told her. "We need to get started right away."

Chapter 12

"Hi, girls," Mrs. Carew said, as Katie and Suzanne ran into Katie's house after school the next day. "Do you want a snack?"

"No thanks, Mom. We've got too much to do," Katie answered.

Mrs. Carew shrugged. "Okay, I have some bills to pay anyway. I'll be in my room if you need me."

Katie waited until her mother was all the way upstairs before she started executing her plan.

"Get the peanut butter from the refrigerator, Suzanne?" Katie asked, finally.

"I thought we didn't have time for a

snack," Suzanne answered.

"It's not for us." Katie bent down and picked up one of Pepper's toy bones.

Pepper sat up tall, waiting. He thought Katie was going to play fetch with him.

No such luck.

"Sorry, boy," Katie told him. "I need to borrow this for someone else."

Katie covered both ends of the bone with peanut butter. Then she stuffed a few of Pepper's treats in her pocket. "Okay, let's go in the backyard," she told Suzanne.

"What are we going to do out there?" Suzanne asked.

Katie smiled. "You'll see."

Katie walked outside and placed the bone on the grass below her backyard deck. Then she walked back over to Suzanne, who was standing near the side of the house.

The girls stared at the bone. They waited.

And waited.

And waited some more.

"Nothing's happening," Suzanne complained.

"It will," Katie assured her. "That bone is perfect."

Suzanne looked curiously at her best friend. "I don't get it. How is a peanut-butter bone going to get Pepper out of trouble?"

Katie pointed to the bone. "That's how."

Suzanne looked where Katie was pointing. There, in the middle of Katie's lawn, sat the little white puppy. Her tail wagged excitedly as she licked the peanut butter from the bone.

"Who's that?" Suzanne asked.

"That's the vegetable thief," Katie answered. She reached into her pocket and pulled out a tasty dog treat.

The white puppy lifted her nose in the air and sniffed. As soon as she spotted Katie, she froze in place. She wasn't sure whether to grab the treat or run away.

The puppy was very hungry, and the treat was very tempting. Finally, the dog scampered over toward Katie. She opened her mouth and snatched the treat from Katie's fingers.

Katie scooped the pup up in her arms and carried her over to the side of the house. "That's a good girl." Katie petted the dog's back gently. "Don't be scared. I want to help you."

The dog struggled for a moment. Katie gave her another treat. The pup calmed down and began to chew.

"Isn't she cute?" Katie asked Suzanne.

Suzanne stared at the scrawny puppy with the dirty, matted fur. She wrinkled up her nose. "That dog stinks."

"I know," Katie agreed. "But we're going to clean her up. And then we're going to teach her a few tricks. When we're finished, *no one* will be able to resist her."

Chapter 13

Katie and Suzanne kept the stray in Suzanne's basement. Mrs. Lock wasn't thrilled about having a dog in the house, but she agreed to let the puppy stay for a few days, if the girls promised to walk her and feed her, as long as Suzanne didn't get too attached to her.

"There's no way we can handle adopting a dog right now," Mrs. Lock told the girls. "I have enough to do with baby Heather."

"We're just watching her for a little while," Suzanne assured her mom.

The girls took good care of the little puppy. They bathed her in the basement sink and made her a bed from a broken bread basket. They fed her and gave her plenty of water.

And every afternoon after school, they worked on training her.

Finally, after about a week, Katie and Suzanne were ready to give the puppy a test. They wanted to see how much she had learned.

Katie stood and looked firmly at the white puppy. "Sit," she said.

The puppy sat up tall.

Katie walked away. "Stay," she ordered.

The puppy stayed right where she was.

Katie sat down on her knees. "Come," she said.

The puppy scampered over to Katie.

"Good girl." Katie handed her a treat. "I think she's ready," she told Suzanne.

"Do you really think this is going to work?" Suzanne asked.

"It just has to," Katie answered.

Katie scooped up the puppy and began walking toward Mrs. Derkmans' house. When they reached their teacher's front door, Katie put the puppy on the porch.

"Stay," she said firmly. Then she rang the doorbell and ran away.

Katie went over to where Suzanne was hiding behind an old tree. Together, the girls watched as the Derkmans' door opened.

Mr. Derkman looked outside. At first he didn't see anyone. Then he noticed the small white puppy.

"Aren't you just the cutest little thing?" He lifted her into his arms. "Kootchy-kootchy-koo."

Katie smiled. At least *Mr.* Derkman liked the puppy.

"Freddy Bear, who is it?" Mrs. Derkman asked, as she came to the door. She saw the dog in her husband's arms. "Oh, no. Where did that thing come from?"

"Someone left her on our doorstep."

"Well, get rid of it. Go call the animal shelter."

"But Snookums, look how cute she is," Mr. Derkman pleaded.

"I don't want to look at her. I want you to get rid of her," Mrs. Derkman insisted.

Katie gulped. Things were not going the way she'd planned. She'd thought her teacher would fall in love with the puppy at first sight. Katie figured that once Mrs. Derkman learned to love dogs, she'd be nicer to Pepper. But that wasn't what was happening at all. Mrs. Derkman hated the dog.

What a mess! First, Pepper had gotten in trouble, and now this poor little dog was going to be sent to a shelter—and it was all Katie's fault.

Suddenly, the puppy picked up her head and licked Mrs. Derkman on the hand.

"Yuck!" the teacher exclaimed. "Dog germs."

Mr. Derkman petted the puppy on the head. "I think she likes you, Snookums," he said.

"Don't be ridiculous," Mrs. Derkman said.

"She wants you to hold her," Mr. Derkman said. "Come on, just for a minute."

Mrs. Derkman sighed. "Fine. For a minute. Then you call the shelter."

Mr. Derkman placed the puppy in his wife's arms. The little dog snuggled up against Mrs. Derkman's shoulder.

The teacher slowly reached up and nervously stroked the puppy's fur. The puppy nuzzled closer against Mrs. Derkman's neck.

Mr. Derkman smiled. "She's awfully cute, Snookums. And she seems to need a home. We could give her a nice home."

Mrs. Derkman sighed. She'd seen that look in her husband's eyes before. There was no fighting him when he wanted something this badly.

"Well, I'm certainly not going to walk her," Mrs. Derkman told her husband.

"I'll do that," Mr. Derkman assured her.

"And I don't have time to brush her or bathe her," Mrs. Derkman continued.

"I'll take care of that," Mr. Derkman said. "I'll take care of everything. All you have to do is enjoy her."

Mrs. Derkman handed the dog over to her husband and shook her head. "That's going to be the hardest part," she said.

Chapter 14

A few mornings later, Katie awoke to a terrible screeching noise.

"How much is that doggie in the window?" Mrs. Derkman sang from her garden.

"Aroo!"

Mrs. Derkman and the dog were singing together! Katie had to see this! She dressed quickly, put Pepper on his leash, and headed outside.

Mrs. Derkman was working in her garden. The white puppy was sitting at her side. Neither the dog nor Mrs. Derkman seemed to notice Katie at first. They were too busy singing.

"There was a teacher, had a dog, and Snowball was her name-oh," Mrs. Derkman sang.

"*Ruff! Ruff!*" Snowball chimed in.

Mrs. Derkman stopped singing when she saw Katie and Pepper. "Hi, Katie," she said cheerfully.

"Hello," Katie said.

"Why don't you bring Pepper over here?" Mrs. Derkman said. "I'd like him to meet Snowball."

Katie was about to tell Mrs. Derkman that Pepper already knew Snowball, but she decided not to. It would be too hard to explain.

"You can take Pepper off the leash if you want," Mrs. Derkman said, as Katie led her dog into the teacher's yard.

Katie looked down as she unhooked Pepper's leash. She could see Snowball happily chomping on a cucumber. Mrs. Derkman didn't seem to mind at all.

"I suppose I owe you and Pepper an apology," Mrs. Derkman said slowly.

Katie didn't know what to say. She'd never heard her teacher apologize to anyone before.

The teacher watched as Pepper and Snowball sniffed each other. "I never dreamed it would be such fun to have a pet," she told Katie. "Snowball seems to like my singing even more than my plants do. And she's more

fun to talk to than Sven was."

Katie was amazed. Having a dog sure had changed Mrs. Derkman. She didn't seem as stern as she did in school.

"Now, don't you think you should go study for that Social Studies test?" Mrs. Derkman continued. "It's going to be very hard."

Okay, maybe she hadn't changed that much.

Katie watched as Pepper and Snowball barked at a squirrel in a tree. The squirrel didn't seem to like being outnumbered.

Katie smiled. It served him right.

"There was a teacher, had a dog, and Snowball was her name-oh," Mrs. Derkman began singing again.

"*Aroo!*" Snowball joined in with a loud howl.

Katie laughed. Having her teacher for a next-door neighbor wouldn't have been something Katie would have wished for. But maybe it wasn't going to be so bad after all.

Chapter 15

It didn't take long for Katie to teach Snowball a few simple tricks. You can teach your dog, too. All you have to do is follow these easy steps.

You will have to practice these tricks alot before your dog will learn them. Some dogs can learn tricks in a few days. It takes other dogs longer to learn.

Teach Your Dog to Sit: This is the easiest trick for your dog to learn. Start by holding a dog treat above her, just out of her reach. Your dog will look up. Then . . . whoops! She'll fall right into the sit position. As soon as your dog begins to fall back, say the word "sit." Then be sure to give your dog a lot of praise—and the treat.

If you do this over and over, your dog will understand what the word "sit" means.

Teach Your Dog to Stay: Start by asking your dog to sit. Then hold your hand out so your palm is near her nose. This is your signal for "stay." Take a step backward, saying the word "stay." Before your dog can move toward you, hurry back to her. Give her a treat.

Repeat this a few times. Each time, move a little farther from your dog. Stay away from her for longer amounts of time, too. She'll soon learn to stay, no matter how far away you may seem.

* * *

Author's note: Katie was very lucky that Snowball was a sweet puppy. But there's no guarantee that other stray dogs are as nice. If you see a strange dog wandering your neighborhood, don't try to rescue her yourself. Instead, ask a grown-up to call a local shelter. They will send an expert to rescue the dog.